For Christopher
Butler this book and
eat it for breakfast
        with
            strawberry jelly!

        C.Drg

Crescent Dragonwagon
Katie in the Morning
Pictures by Betsy Day

Harper & Row

Katie in the Morning
Text copyright © 1983 by Crescent Dragonwagon
Illustrations copyright © 1983 by Betsy Day

Library of Congress Cataloging in Publication Data
Dragonwagon, Crescent.
    Katie in the morning.

    Summary: Katie revels in the solitude of an early-
morning walk before the rest of her family wakes.
    [1. Solitude–Fiction]   I. Day, Betsy A., ill.
II. Title.
PZ7.D7824Kat 1983   [E]   82-47709
ISBN 0-06-021729-4
ISBN 0-06-021730-8 (lib. bdg.)

For Marilyn Marlow, who,
in her caring for her clients,
is a morning person
and an afternoon person
and an evening person

This morning, I opened my eyes
and was awake, all at once,
and knew I was the first,
the only one awake in the still house,
the quiet house,
shadowed because the sun wasn't full up
and no one was moving yet,
not even me.
Then I moved
and the day was mine!

Creep-creep-creeping down the stair
past Mama and Daddy and my brother Henry
past them all, past them, creeping secret away
no one to stop me and no one to say
"Who's there?" or "Where are you going?
When will you be back?"
The day was mine.

Pulling on jeans and a sweat shirt,
two slim dimes from the kitchen basket in my pocket;
blue sneakers on, and pulling tight the fat yellow laces,
tying them and flying away!
The day was mine,
mine and the honeysuckle sweeting down
the mist-filled morning air.

And there,
walking under the trees,
I saw a cat
in brilliant black and white
against the wet green leaves:

8

complacent cat,
satisfied cat,
sitting, one paw up, licking it.
She blinked at me.

Is she waiting for the sun to warm her?
What blue bowl did she lick cream out of,
licking and licking,
right down to the empty shining china?
A cup of cream, a pint, a quart?
Or is it just that morning's *hers*
that makes her smirk?
She blinked at me, that cat.
I don't know whose she is.
She doesn't know whose I am, either:
this morning, each our own.
Two morning sailors, she and I,
out to sail the day.
We blinked and sailed away.

My feet went crunch crunch crunch
on the red-clay gravel road.
It had rained the night before, and bits of clay
stuck to the waffled bottoms of my shoes.
I breathed in more and more,
and walked with purpose.
I made as much or little sound as I liked!
This time was mine!

Crunch crunch crunch.
(They won't deliver, not down *this* lumpy bumpy road,
that's what the man told Daddy.)

And then I hunched up the hill to the highway,
through the green gloom of the misty woods,
a piney cave—
look, at the top—

the wild roses are in bloom! And smell!

Sniff-sniff-sniffing through the air
honeysuckle, roses, pine, and rain
in my nose and in my brain
in my fingers, in my hair
in my step and in my walk
in the way the cardinals talk,
singing, "Pretty, pretty, pretty,"
to each other, across the valley.

Red as blood they were,
bright splashes on a leafy branch.
There were two
on the telephone wire
as I mounted
the top of the hill.

I walked up the carless gray highway,
past the quiet playground,
the swings and seesaws empty
and still and dew covered,
the iris in a clump
like a flock of small pale yellow birds
caught in flight.
Soon cars would whoosh by
and children play and fight
and iris bend in the afternoon wind
but then, so still.

"Pretty, pretty, pretty,"
called the cardinals,
combining with a million other birdsongs
whose words I didn't know yet, but someday will
in the morning of a day that's mine.
Mine alone—yet with two thin silver dimes,
secret ordinary moons,
in my own pocket . . .

Freed's Market at the top of the hill, still closed;
oranges and apples in wooden crates
gleamed like planets in the half-dark of the unlit shop.
But out front—
the four-legged red metal newspaper box
was waiting and full.
I slipped my dimes in the slot and it unlocked.
I opened it, and slid out a newspaper, folded,
never read by anyone.
I tucked it under my arm
and turned toward home.

Walking back,
I knew that Mama and Daddy and
my brother Henry were groggy, stirring now,
splashing water on sleepy faces
groaning awake into clothes
starting coffee with its sharp brown steamy smell.

I knew, when I came in, that Daddy would say, yawning,
"It's our Katie-bird, Earlybird!
Where did you fly off to, Katie-bird?"
And Mama would kiss me and say,
"Good morning, sweetie, thanks for getting the paper!
Two pieces of French toast for you, or three?"
And Henry would only say, "Comics."

And Daddy would say, "What I want to know is, how come this family of owls got lucky and wound up with an earlybird to take care of us?" And Henry would say, "What I want to know is, how can she STAND to get up so early?"

And that's what they all said.

How could I tell them
that morning is my blue bowl of cream?
I lift it and tilt it
and drain the last drop.
I drink it down.
I lick my lips, and blink.